Stories from the Sacred Hoop of Life

Ron Henderson
Stories from the Sacred Hoop of Life

Published by BooxAi

ISBN: 978-965-577-943-1

Stories from the Sacred Hoop of Life

Ron Henderson

CONTENTS

1. Juggernaut 7
2. Tsu-na-mi (Warning) 9
3. Captain 11
4. Oak Tree 15
5. Falling Rocks 17
6. Two Face (Janus) 21
7. Transit Station 23
8. Eventful Day 25
9. The Princessa and sea shell 31
10. The Alchemist and The Hypnotist 43

JUGGERNAUT

It was 1939, I was just a wee pup, on a farm in Kansas, sitting on the porch with my mama shelling pea's, she in her rocking chair, me in a porch swing; swinging back in forth, and our old coon dog listening to her talk about the old days. When suddenly everything grew silent, and still, an eerie feeling, not a sound on the farm, when suddenly that was shattered by my father's distant voice as he ran from the barn yelling, "Ellie and Sam, get to the storm cellar," we took off running, that coon dog fast behind barking; and it seemed that just then the air got thin, hard to breathe as we reached the cellar double doors. I could see particles floating in the air as I started to hear the sound of a train that is fast approaching, so loud I couldn't even hear my thoughts, or that coon dog, who just kept on yelping. And hours later, as we stepped out of the cellar, everything for miles around, even our farm, had been swept away. I heard them say on the radio, calling the thing a Juggernaut. I learned in school later on that's something that crushes everything in it's way, an advancing force. But most people around my part's just called it a tornado, even to this day when that coon dog hears a train, it scares him, and me too. Yep, that was in 1939, yep 1939...

Tsu-na-mi (Warning)

Once a very long time ago in a oceanside village there lived a young girl, who was born with a deformity that left her face disfigured. She was always shunned and teased by others in the village, especially the other children. So she was very lonely, but she loved her village and her land, for she would explore the hills, and sea shore alone often, experiencing it's majestic beauty. She also likes to listen to the old stories that the elderly villager's would tell. One was about, once in a great season, the earth would shake, and the sea would send a great wave to take the village's away. And that made the girl sad, for she loved her village even though it treated her bad. Then one day, the earth shook violently, and the young girl ran to the sea shore rocks seeing the ocean swell, started crying "I'm so lonely, I'm so lonely, I'm so lonely, take me, take me," some of the villager's deep in fear heard the crying, and ran to see that the young girl was standing on the sea shore edge, and watched as the great ocean swell rose, and snatched the young girl off the edge of the ocean rocks, and then receded back into it's place saving the villagers. Now until this day, when the earth shakes, the people near the sea cry out the girl's name "Tsunami, Tsunami," to warn that the great wave may come, so run to high ground...Song: I used to watch her stand on the cliff by the sea, looking out into the mystery of the ocean void. She stood there morning, noon, and at the sunset evening tide. Sending prayers on the wind, just as the seagulls fly, seeking healing for some of life's despairs. Then one day the earth shook as it could feel her pain. And as the tide pulled back, you could hear her say "I'm so lonely, I'm so lonely, take me away from this place," and as the ocean stretched forth it's mighty hand to free her from the lone-liness and pain.

And when you shake, and deep inside you feel life's pain. Let the sea pull back and stretch forth it's mighty healing hand and free you from the sadness and pain.

CAPTAIN

It's a chill night, and I'm warming my hands by the campfire I just started, it's slow to get going because the only wood branches I could collect have moss on them, it's a slow smoky start, but the warmth is starting to grow, others now come in closer to warm their hands and bodies, it's been a long ride. I'm assigned the duty of making the fire pit, a duty I am privileged to do, that and bed, and feed the horses. The Natives say the fire keeper is an important member of the tribe to be looked up to; for the fire keeper brings the power of warmth, and light to it's people. It's been burning a good while now, and the men have put a coffee kettle on the hot rocks by the fire pit, and venison that was caught earlier in the day roasting on a split-stick over the fire. As we surround the fire pit listening to the Captain speak, I kneel to warm my hands as I put my carbine over my shoulder, I listen to the Captain's words mesmerized. It is said he has a messianic aura when he speaks, it's an honor for me to be here at this moment in this time; the

Captain calls it zeitgeist, the spirit of the time, and now the moment is upon us to change the hands of destiny in what we must do. I am only eighteen, the youngest among us, the Captain has allowed me to *come* for I believe in his cause, also I'm his son, but even if I wasn't, I would follow this man to the death. As he continues to speak, he and some of his commanders look over charts, and maps instructing us all on our tactical strategies and positions. As I look around into each man's eyes, I can see the discipline and loyalty in their faces. Each man will follow the captain's orders without question, each prepared to sacrifice his life. The Captain runs his camp under stern discipline, each man is of the highest moral character, there is no swearing, no alcohol, or unruly conduct, no cowardice in attitude, each man and woman is treated equally without regards to color, status, or servitude. The Captain governs his army on the philosophical principals of Biblical scriptures and prayer. And now as we sit around the fire, some of us know this may be our last time hearing his prophetic words, someone starts to sing softly: "one day early I started on my journey walking the road of life. I met a man they called Captain, a preacher who said he fought for freedom, and as he started to speak I had to bow on my knees and humble myself to a righteous power greater than me. He told me his story of his struggle to set all men free, I ask him can I join him for this too I believed. And on one very cold night we plotted to fight, sitting by a fire down at the cold river. As I listen to the words he speaks, telling me of his mission, I feel a sensation warming me as he said these things, and I thank God for allowing his light to shine forth upon me.

Now as I look down into the reflection of the water, I see my life in front of me, and I can feel the breeze blowing on my face, as I stand by the cold, cold river. And as the river rushes past, and I can see that time won't last, for the day that I die, my story will be that they buried me by a tree where I met a preacher named Captain who baptized me down by the cold, cold river". And as we continue to listen to his eloquent message, we know this mission we do is for righteous cause and purpose. As we mount the horses and prepare to ride out, the Captain, my father looks me in the eye, and I know that there's no other place in life that I rather be than by Captain Commander John Brown side, as we ride towards Harper's ferry...

OAK TREE

On a cold winter's day as a blizzard wind sweeps through my house, my wife and child sit in a chair looking out the window with a hungry stare. As I look to the hearth into the fire place where no fire's burn. And I envision the black emptiness, it hurts to see how I let my family come to despair. I grab an ax and head out the door into the winter's embrace, but as I step on the solid ground I can hear my father's voice whisper from distant past, "before you walk out that door to cut down that old oak tree, remember how it stood for you and me, it gave you shelter in the shade on those hot, hot summer day's whistle in it's leaves as the wind blows it's breeze. Just remember that when you walk out into the yard to cut down that old oak tree. Remember how good it was to you and to me. The time when you use to chase that little girl with pig tales around that tree counting, one, two, three, my love for you; your love for me, early mornings just as the sun begins it's rise, the harmony of the Birds singing the sounds of joy for the coming of another day. Remember as a child building the house of your dreams in that tree, looking into the theater of a night sky; seeing the celestial dancer's of star's showing you your destiny in life. So think in gratitude when you grab that ax and walk out that door to cut down that old oak tree, remember how it stood for you and me. How it stood in the storms through the mighty wind's and rains. Shedding it's leaves each season letting you know that time's do change, each ring around it's core showing you there's growth even through pain. And remember the time you put your child in the seat of life to push him on the swing that still hangs from that tree, just as your father pushed you to grow, to swing to heights you thought you'd never see. Now even in times of trouble, hunger, and hurt, you need it's wood as fuel to burn in the fire for comfort and warmth, just remember that as you walk out that door to cut down that old oak tree. Now as I, my wife and child sit around the fire place singing and smiling as food cooks over the fire, I feel the warmth of the fire, and as I look into the ember's I can see the love and happiness in my families eye's. And as I turn to look outside my window, I can still see I didn't have to cut it down, just removed a few of it's many limbs that stretch forth their hands, because it's roots run deep. I will always remember how it stands for you and me.

FALLING ROCKS

Two Native Indian Braves wanted to marry a very beautiful girl, Blossom, the Chief's daughter. Two young braves one named Running Fast, because he was always first, and pride himself at being the best at everything, the second Braves name was Falling Rocks, because when he was a toddler he once climbed up a hill and there he dislodged some rocks that came rolling down the hill. They both wanted to marry Blossom, but one was deeply in love with her, and he was falling rock, he had deeply fallen in love with Blossom, at an early age they always played together, and he knew she was both beautiful and intelligent, Running Fast like Blossom because of her beauty, and cause she was the tribal chiefs daughter, and marrying her would guarantee tribal status, and surly chieftainship. Both went to the chief Gray Owl to state their attentions, chief Gray Owl said the only way to wed his daughter is whoever brings the best gift. So both set out to find and bring back the best gift. Three days passed with anticipation for Blossom wanted it to be Falling Rock, for deep within her heart she had a place for him. On the fourth day Running Fast returns first with many ponies, and for an Indian Brave ponies as a gift, could not be topped for ponies to the tribe are the best asset, and achievement next to showing bravery in battle. Falling Rock hadn't returned in over a week, Blossom becomes sick with fever, the chief sends out a search party to find Falling Rock. And even to this day, as I am driving, I can still see signs saying "Watch Out for Falling Rocks." Now, when I first heard this story I laughed real hard, but I said to myself is that it? What happens to Falling Rock, what becomes of Blossom? The search party searched for days finding no trail, no sign. Blossom becomes sicker, decaying, preparing to sing the death song, other's in the tribe become ill also, with the same sickness. No one could find Falling Rock, for he had been on a seven day vision quest, a powerful sacred Native ceremony of fasting, and mental, and physical perseverance. His vision spirit told him he had to travel to a distant mountain to find his gift.

Along his quest he had to endure a torrential rain storm, having to swim a rising river. Walking for miles through a long hot desert, while encountering a wolf he had to slay, and skinned for it's fur. Even though Falling Rock knew he had been gone for a while and that Running Fast may have married Blossom, he followed his vision as he was told to do. He now came to a mountain and had to climb a rocky hillside, a most dangerous challenge for its possibility of a rock slide, he climbed successfully without causing any rocks to fall. At the top of the mountain there was a meadow full of plants and flowers. In his vision he was to pick certain types of plant herbs and return to his tribe. It took days for him to return back home; but early one morning walking into the tribe he felt sadness, for many looked sick and weak, and as tribe member's recognized him, word started to spread that Falling Rock had returned. He went immediately to chief Grey Owl's tipi, to present his gift, knowing Blossom was already married but what he found instead was sadness, for Blossom lay weak and frail.

Chief Grey Owl explained what had happened in his absence and told him Running Fast declined to marry Blossom, he had lost interest after she had become sick, he felt she was less than beautiful now saying she had become withered, and that he brought the best gift for the best wife. Falling Rock went to Blossom's side, and she managed to smile, Falling Rock said "no matter if you had married Running Fast, my gift to you would be that you have happiness, and a long life, for I have known you all my life; and you have always been the sunlight that enlightens my day, and blossomed the love in my heart." At that moment he reached in his bag pulling something out saying "on my journey this is all that I was able to get, for the spirit in me told me this is what I needed to get. The chief and the medicine man looked at the herb's he had brought, and had them cured for use. In a healing ceremony this herb tea was given to the whole tribe, including Blossom, it was a remedy for sickness that had spread. The tribe thanked Falling Rock for he had truly brought the best gift; that of healing of the community, and in a wonderful ceremony he married Blossom who recovered into a beautiful flower, later he became chief, with the name of Standing Rock..

TWO FACE (JANUS)

Janus: god of gates, and door's of all beginnings, Roman mythology two opposite faces.

Two men locked in a prison cell looking out through window bars. One looking down only saw mud. The other looking up only saw the star's...Dale Carnagie (How to win friends and influence people)

Cry for all the memories and experiences missed. Opportunities and achievements lost in a foggy mist. Time swept away incarcerated like a encapsulated ship in a bottle long forgotten thought's left dusting on a shelf, fading hopes and dreams falling like leaves in an ending season of death. Many storms raging through life, mighty winds blow across the sand and seas through the lonely desert of the mind. But just as the sunrises a new day will dawn, spring comes around, good wine matures with time, and things do change. Inspiration shines through the darkness of night like a ray of sun light into the depths of the soul. Just like rain drops from the sky, the tears fall from the eyes washing away the stains from the heart giving a breath of life, that is the freedom of air beneath open wings that let's creativity fly as high as it ascends to be free as it was created perfectly to be, that is the most glorious gift to receive. Two men locked in a prison cell looking out through window bars, one looking down only saw mud, the other looking up seeking the stars. Which one will you be the choice is only yours. Don't cry for all the memories and experiences missed, take command of destiny ship and chart your future course on the seven seas of success. One man with two faces but yet one heart. Which one will you choose, the choice is only yours if you just look and seek...

Transit Station

I left home one day walking to the transit station, and as I approached the platform, a stunningly attractive young lady with an open smile, and inviting presents, was standing there, and I was about to ask her a question, and her name, the train arrived, and she boarded; but just before the doors were about to close, I yelled out "what is your name?" She yelled back in response " Opportunity!" As the transit door's shut, and as I stood on that lonely platform dejected and sad, there was music playing from the transit address system (walk on by, by Dionne Warrick). And as I watched the train left the station moving forward, with opportunity aboard, I walked away with my head down defeated, but a spark of light within my heart, led me to return each day at the same time wanting to get a glimpse, to see her again. Then one day when I was at my lowest point, wanting to give up, commit suicide, I saw her standing there on the transit platform, and as I ran to approach her and as my vision cleared, I could see someone was also there with her. I wanted to talk with her, but I could see she was involved, so I just said hi, she spoke and introduced her companion, as Preparation, he and I struck up a conversation, and he invited me to meet him later on, he became a friend and mentor; for he was a personal trainer and started me to work out with exercise and discipline, encouraging me, building my self-esteem, and sense of purpose, and during this training I started to run, developing my wind, then I started to run a marathon, and while running I bumped into an extraordinarily beautiful woman, whose eye's sparkled with inspiration and magnetism, and as we looked into each other's eyes I felt an enchanting feeling. I asked her name, she said "Serendipity" and started to jog along side of me, motivating me in area's I never knew, and as we ran along the path, my perception became better. I started to see things along the pathway more clearly, and my mind and endurance increased and became better. Now with her by my side I started to win my contest and challenges with comfort and confidence. We got married and from that magical union we had a wonderful child and named it "Success".

EVENTFUL DAY

One morning two people left on a journey, one seeking thrill and adventure, the other seeking to end their life. A very prominent millionaire left home enthusiastic, and feeling great for today was going to be a breath taking sight hiking a popular trail to go mountain climbing. Something he had been looking forward to for weeks; his business was successful and he had finalized a major deal to expand his company. Also, his wife had just had their second child. So climbing this mountain was going to be a welcomed accomplishment. He had packed a hefty backpack with all the needed necessities for once at the top of the mountain he would camp, and spend the night under the star's and hike down the next morning. It was a beautiful day, crispy air, translucent skies, and he started off at a good pace, if he kept it up he would reach the bottom of the mountain by noon, just before one in the afternoon, he was at the bottom of the mountain, but he wanted to save time, so he decided to take a steeper route up the side of the mountain, so he started the climb. It was a breath taking view with a steep ascent up, half way up, he came to a difficult area, for the rains had eroded the soil in area's where rocks were on the topside of the mountain, having dislodged a rock as he stepped in an area that had loose soil, it began to slide, causing him to fall down the side of the mountain off a cliff into a ravine severely injuring himself with a broken leg, and head concussion, he yelled out in pain causing him to blackout. At the same time that the millionaire started his hike, another person started their journey also, but this journey was less enthusiastic, in fact it was a death walk, for it was a young woman who was depressed and lonely, having lost her fiance in a car crash, a year before, and six months later losing the child she had been caring. She felt she couldn't go living in this life anymore, without the one person she loved, and loved her, and not having a child to share it with. So she decided to hike and climb the favorite mountain they had both climbed many times before armed only with a picture of her fiance, and a farewell letter, she started to climb, for she knew of a deep ravine that she would plunge off into from the top of the mountain. She was alone, and wanted to die alone in the beauty of silence, on a bright clear day, so she took the long way up for she had love to climb, and hike this mountain with her fiance, so she would savor it's majestic beauty one more time taking the long trail up. As she started her hike she thought of the words of Wordsworth: "Earth has not anything to show more fair: Dull would he be of soul who could pass by a sight so touching in it's majesty" (1802). She reflected on many things in her life as she ascended up the mountain, reaching the top and now standing at the edge of the cliff, just above the ravine.

She surveyed the panoramic beauty of the place she and her fiance had shared many times for the last time, as she took it in and was about to jump, she heard a painful cry. For at that moment, the millionaire had come too, crying out for help, knowing no one would hear his cry, in the isolated area. But, in the distance he heard a response. "Where are you, is anyone out there?" He yelled "yes" "I'm down here in the ravine, I'm badly hurt, and need your help." She responds, "I'm up on top of the cliff, it will take me a while to safely get down to you, hold on." He responds "please hurry!" It takes her over an hour to get to where he had fallen. Reaching him, she sees how badly his injuries are. She sees he's in a lot of pain, and needs serious medical attention, for he has a very bad broken leg, and from the wound on his head, and incoherence that it would be diffi-cult to move him, she thinks, should she go for help? She decides it's too risky, for it's almost dark, and with the drop in temperature and possibility of wild animals, she can't leave him to go for help, so with the little first aid she knows and the few supplies he has in his backpack, she stabilizes him the best she can, gets fresh water from the small stream that is at the bottom of the ravine, she makes a fire and tries to comfort him the best she can, he is still in a lot of pain, but speaking more coherently now, it's a good sign. They formally introduce themselves, he tells her of his life, and how he came to be on the mountain today, she just tells him she had hiked this mountain a few times her, and her fiance, but didn't share her reason, just moving on to the subject of what best to do to get him out of the ravine, and medical help for his injuries. They decide the only way, and the best way is for him to be carried out, as soon as possible. It's decided, it's too dark now, and both need rest, for she has to build a make shift travois to pull down the mountain trail. They sleep, with the fire still burning. The early morn comes quick, she sets out immediately to construct the travois, having completed this, she secures him in, and they start the trek down the mountain. It's a hard, difficult process, for the weight and the terrain make it rough, but he's conscious, and in pain, but talkative, to keep his mind off the pain, and to motivate her, because he could see the strain she is enduring to get him out, but being a good judge of people, he suspects something was bothering her, so he bluntly asked her, what's troubling her, he's thinking that his condition is worse than she has revealed.

The weight was too heavy for her to bear, not just the physical weight of him on the travois, but the emotional pain, suffering, and loneliness she had been enduring. So she breaks down stopping setting down the travois, finally releasing the hurtful load crying uncontrollably, she explains her life and the true reason she was standing at the top of the mountain. He listened for a long while, she finishes he's silent for a moment, then he speaks. He starts with a quote by Von ave Hartmann (1170-1215) "He who helps in saving others, saves himself as well." Then he goes on to say, he can't judge her for her decision, for at a point in his life, he had lost everything wealth, and health, he had once had cancer and given six months to live. Then he read a book "Man's search for meaning" by Victor Frankl. And realized that life is a gift in everything, even though we suffer loss, hurt, adversity, it's still a gift given to us, to use our best potential, to help others that may not have the means to help themselves like the situation they are now in, if she had jumped off that cliff, he would not have the needed help to be able to have a chance to survive. No amount of wealth or fame could he use in this situation, just the unselfish sacrifice of another human being to his aid. There is a touching spirit that flows through life as a river at times manipulating peoples mind, circumstances, and situations, that create miraculous changes in people's lives for the greater and common good. So realize your life is a precious gift, to you even though you lost your husband, and unborn child, think about all the lonely, unwanted, abused children that need your love, and care, also there is someone lonely out there, that would benefit greatly from your friendship, and I'm one of them. With that they both walked down the mountain with a new outlook on life. Looking into the beautiful day with new possibilities. "So it is more useful to watch a man in times of peril, and adversity to discern what kind of man he is; for then at last words of truth are drawn from the depths of his heart, and the mask is torn off, reality remains"... Lucetius (99-55 B.C)

THE PRINCESSA AND SEA SHELL

In a kingdom by the sea, there lived a princessa with her royal family and it's citizens. The people of this kingdom were beautiful and happy for their country flourished with riches of trade, and culture, because it was a kingdom by the ocean, and a popular trade route. It was known to be ruled by a just king that was wise and fair to all his guest, and subject's. The king and queen had one child, the princessa, who they both loved, and showed much affection. The princessa loved to walk along the sea shore, which gave her peace and joy. One day she was walking along the shore after a big storm had passed the night before, she saw something in the cove; for the tide had receded, when she got closer she saw that it was a person, she ran towards the person, as she approached her eyes grew with amazement, for what she saw she only heard in folktales, it was a mermaid that laid lifeless, but upon closer inspection she could see that she still breathed. From the folktales she had heard that mermaids could not live outside water, she could see that this mermaid was in need of water, so she dragged the mermaid to a near by cove, into water; slowly the mermaid came to consciousness. At first the mermaid was startled, but the princessa communicated to her that she was there to help her; but strangely and wondrously she could understand the mermaids thought's and feeling's without speaking a word. the mermaid introduced herself Nerissa, and they were able to communicate through the power of the heart, using telepathy, she told her how she got caught by the powerful storm on the ocean. The mermaid said that she was too weak to swim back out into the ocean and find her family. She needed time to heal, and needed the princessa secrecy not to tell a soul that she was there in the cave. The princessa promised her she would keep the secret, and would come each day to help her heal. The princessa returned to the castle, talking to the wise counsel of the court and reading in the library all the information she could about the stories of mermaids.

Meanwhile, her father had taken counsel on a political matter of foreign concerns, a king from a far off land who had come to great prominence through war's, and battle's conquering lands and kingdoms; he had sent an emissary to the king requesting he give over his trade routes, those trade routes had been prosperous and known for over a thousand year's making his kingdom wealthy, productive, and famous. He couldn't just give over these routes, but he knew if he didn't, that war would surely be declared upon his kingdom. Although his kingdom was known to be defender's of good, and peace, winning many battle's. The king knew the opposing king was merciless, slaughtering countless innocent and destroying life. The king did not want his people to have to endure such malice, but he was righteous and just and could not give up his people livelyhood of the trade route's he would have to think of a solution. His trusted advisors suggested, that if an ample gift of generosity was offered, an alliance could be formed and war avoided. The king asked what suggestion did they mean? The advisors spoke of the law of all the kingdoms, if a member of a royal family marries someone of royal Birth, or honor, of another land, or kingdom then a peace alliance is created. The advisors said that the king would have to give his daughter in marriage to the kings son, this suggestion upset the king for, if the king of that kingdom was such a tyrant, then his son could only be a tyrant too. The counsel explained to the king, that the only other option would be a long drawn out war, that thousands would die, and other's would suffer for years to come, commerce and prosperity would soon cease. The king said he would have to retire for the evening alone, to contemplate on the decision he would have to make. Later as he stood on the balcony of his castle, looking out to the sea as the sun was beginning to set, he could see his daughter princessa walking along the shore of the beach as she returned from her walk of solitude, that he knew she enjoyed so much. As she came closer to the castle, he went to meet her. As he approached her on the sandy shore, she saw him and ran towards him beaming with a smile of joy. He beamed delightedly also, for he loved his daughter, he inquired about her day, and her walk. She responded "with adventure," he told her he wanted to speak to her and informed her as to the political situation and his dilemma; and it seemed that just then princessa could see the weight of the situation made him seem to age a hundred years. Then looking into his daughter's eye's he said, no matter if he had to battle a thousand years, and countless number's had to die, he wouldn't send his gift away, or that of any of his just and righteous subjects to the suffering life of aggression, and chaos, for the principals of goodness, and truth far outweigh anything and are worth fighting for he explained the dilemma of the political situation and weight of a decision that rested upon him, he watched his daughter's expression as he shared his thought's with her, he had always confided in her with counsel, for she was a princessa, and needed to understand the complexities of judgment that had to go into rulership of a kingdom. The king knew his daughter was wise beyond her year's, for what she said next hurt him; but also made him proud. To deprive the prosperity of wealth, and peace, to separate families causing war, and destruction to a kingdom, for the selfishness of one, would Be a most egregious travesty, if it means the peace and tranquility will continue to reign the land, I will gladly sacrifice. So the decree was made, and emissaries dispatched. In the following week's the offer was excepted by the tyrant king. Before the princessa was to make her long journey, she took her a walk along the ocean shore, making her way to the cove, to see her friend the mermaid, for now she was healthy and ready to journey back to sea to reunite with her family, she knew of the princessa's situation and knew she had to leave. Since it would be her last time maybe seeing her, and how she would miss the sea they both stood in the ocean water looking out to sea, and as the tide pulled back to expose the sea floor, the mermaid picked up a sea shell, handing it to the princessa, telling her no matter where she will travel, or how far she shall go; if she puts the sea shell against her heart, she will feel the ocean waves, with the vibrations of her heart, if she places it by her nose she will smell the fragrance of the ocean's salt, and if she holds it near her ear she will hear the harmony of the sound's of the sea. The princessa thanked her for her gift and told the mermaid that she would truly miss their friendship, the mermaid informed him that their friendship would transcend the sands of time as she began to say goodbye, heading out to sea. Off shore a school of dolphins awaited to escort the mermaid home. She explained as she swam out that the dolphins are the emissaries of the sea, they will always protect you and guide you to safety. With those last words she disappeared under a wave. The princessa walked away back towards the castle with the sea shell in her hand. The journey to the new land was long, sad, and distant, through desert and over mountains she arrived at the tyrant king's who welcomes her, but explains that his son the prince was off on a short journey, and would be back soon. In fact the prince had purposely left, so as to not be there when the princessa arrived. When his father had informed him of what he was forced to do he became upset, for he was not like his father, arrogant, despotic, evil; in fact he was just the opposite, diplomatic, tolerant, kind hearted and intelligent. His father had ruled through conquering and fear. The prince was a just, and great warrior, that many trusted his leadership and judgment in battle, in which he had now been called off too. When his father informed him of a marriage arrangement, he was not even given any consideration as to what he thought, it was during this that he learned through his father's military counsel that one of the king's many enemies had attacked a peaceful community village unprovoked, only because it resided in the king's providence. The king knew of this but was unconcerned, for the village to him had no strategic value, and the attack was more a minor nuisance to him than a real matter, but to the prince the village had a community of peaceful productive citizen's that lived in accordance to the king's law's he had visited the village many times without escort, or without the citizens knowing of his royalty.

Now that he had come to the village defense, routed, and defeated the enemy attacker's, the villager's recognized him and thanked him; even more so now that they knew he was the prince. Now returning to the castle, he broke away from the escort and wanted time to solus in the forest. He rode his horse to the stream to water it, and there at the edge of the stream, upon a rock sat a extremely beautiful woman, exuded an exotic air, about her, he just stood and watched for a moment, he saw that she had something in her hand, he walked his horse to the edge of the stream a few yards away from her; he water's his horse, and strokes it softly, brushing him slowly. She looks up and smiles, standing up approaching them, saying what a beautiful stallion. He thanks her; and tells her the horse's name, and it's rare Arabian breed. She says she knows and has ridden them before. As she steps forth to stroke the horse, the prince breaks the silence by telling her as he approached the stream, he saw her there holding something in her hand; which she still held. She explained it was a sea shell. The prince said that he had seen them before and had sailed the ocean before. The princessa explained that the sea shell had special powers, magical, that if you place the shell upon your heart, you could feel the motion of the ocean, and the gentleness of the tide, and that if you put the shell to your ear, you can hear the sounds of the sea, and the silence of the waves. She also told him the magic only works if you have an honest and gentle heart. She explained that she used to go to the ocean shore often to see it's beauty and contemplate her thought's as she was doing today, sitting on a rock at the edge of this stream. Thinking of the decision she made in order to save and protect other's, she would have to sacrifice her freedom and dreams.

The prince told her he often came to this same spot for contemplation and reflection and that he too was making a decision he did not want; too, based on the decision making of other's. He asked the princessa, could he touch and hold the shell, hoping that maybe it would help him reflect on the choice he would have to make. Holding the shell, and looking at its fascinating blend of colors, he first placed it on his chest, a very powerful, and overwhelming feeling of a wave of flowing emotion came upon him just as a wave splashes upon shore. He then placed the shell near his ear and the harmony of sounds being both distant, clear, and near, as if one was floating on the ocean's surface. He returned the shell to the princessa hand's and smiled. It now had become late, and the sun was setting, and time to get back to the castle. He thanked the princessa and told her he enjoyed their meeting, and that he came to this stream often; and hoped to see and talk with her again. Mounting his horse before he rode off, he said that the sea shell was a special gift that had been given to her, and to cherish it; with that he left. Each of them returned to the castle separately at different times, retiring to sleep with their own thoughts. The next morning the royal court was called, and introductions were made. As the assembly was called, the king sat in position, with his son next to him, the guest was introduced to the court, and the princessa was introduced to the court as she made her way to the front of the court. Both the princessa and the prince recognized each other from the encounter at the stream the day before, both kind of smiled, but still lost in their own thought's, after formally being introduced, they were sat side, by side, and finally had a chance to exchange words to each other alone, both smiling and questioning why either didn't inform each other of there status, each saying they felt no need to do so. Each agreeing that it had been best, for if they had royal arrogance, and protocol would have caused them not to speak to each other, allowed them to share a moment of magic. As the court banquet proceeded into the evening, one of the king's military dispatchers had returned from a distant outpost, informing the king that his adversaries had now joined together and started to attack and claim territory to conquer, and defeat him. Most of these adversaries had once been peaceful countries until the king's brutal reign. Now the king became very angry and irritated that these submissive ruler's would rise against him, and he wanted personally to subdue them back into submission. He decided that he himself would lead his military into battle, and would leave his son to monitor the kingdom. He left for the journey, as days went by in the king's absence the princessa, and the prince would often walk through the forest, or ride horses to the stream, to dialogue and debate philosophical, cultural, and political issues. The prince could see that the princessa was a very intelligent woman, who was very knowledgeable in many area's of science, arts, history and everyday life issues. He had never met anyone that was well rounded outside of the scholar's in the royal academic court. This intrigued him very much, on the other hand, the princessa found herself conflicted, she wanted to hate, distrust this foreign, unfamiliar place, but being around the prince sharing and discussing ideas, thoughts, and arguments of intellect with this person, who's

father was a exact antithesis of what she lived for, and her principals stood for, but this young man she had time to watch and
see inside his heart having many attributes that her father exhib-
ited. And didn't the sea shell touch him through his heart and
sing to his ear's? Someone like this couldn't possibly be like his
father, a tyrant. Plus she still missed home. As the days went by
a messenger returned bringing the news that the king was killed
in a battle. Ironically there wasn't a lot of mourning, most were
more worried what would happen now. Kingdom law state's
that the rulership was to pass to the prince, the next in line. But
the prince didn't want to rule a kingdom as his father did, and
needed to give it some thought, especially with the political
turmoil that his father had created due to his abuse and rulership over the kingdom for many years. He decided he would
escort the princessa back home, since now she was not under
any obligation to fulfill. He would decide what to do about the
kingdom and the war that was going on when he returned. The
return journey home for the princessa was not long; for now she
looked for it with anticipation. As they arrived she could see the
coast line coming into view and smell the sweet season of the
ocean salt. When they arrived at the castle, the king and queen
awaited their daughter with open arm's. The prince was introduced and greeted with a royal hug, which surprised him. The
queen and the princessa excused themselves to retire until later,
also to get the princessa settled and catch upon royal gossip and
hear about her journey. But the queen was most curious to
know, was about the prince. Meanwhile the king got acquainted
with the prince and discussed the on going turmoil and insta-
bility in his kingdom, they also discussed the loss of his father.
The prince stated that he didn't agree with his father's rulership

or politics, that he didn't want to follow in his footsteps, and that his kingdom may be better off under someone else's rule.

But the prince said it was time to be honest with himself, and now confess to the king. He had escorted the princessa back home to see that she made it safely, but also, to ask her father for her hand in marriage, for all the years of his life, over the many miles and journeys he has traveled no other beauty in life form could compare to the princessa, in intelligence, kindness, and inspiration. These qualities he wanted to share and cherish with her in this life time. The king was impressed by the prince's integrity in words and thoughts at his age. And his humility to ask for the king's authority and blessing in matrimony with his daughter. The king's reply was you have my sincere blessing, but there's only one person's approval you need that counts and that's the princessa's. That afternoon the two both went to stroll the sea shore, walking all the way to the cove where the princessa and the mermaid used to spend time together. There off the shore in the surf they could see dolphins playing in unison.

The prince spoke, I can see why you missed this place it has an enchanting effect, just as you have become from the first moment I saw you as a beam of sunlight upon a rock, cooled by the running spring. You have enchanted my heart, inspired my dreams, captured my thoughts, and subjugated my love. I want to continue this journey in life, but only with you by my side. Princessa, will you walk this journey with me? The princessa spoke slow and softly. When I first traveled to your land, my mind and heart were in a state of contradiction for my principals, morality, and justice stood bulwark against the method's and practice's of brutality, abuse and rulership your father subjected his citizens to, but my heart compels me to make the sacrificing decision to agree to a royal marriage that would prevent war, loss, and suffering to my people, these feelings, thoughts conflicted within me, deep until I met a man, I have *come* to know through actions and deeds to possess attributes of character, courage, sincerity, honesty, and humility, to show me that even in the midst of chaos, oppression, and aggression, the light of truth can shine through the flame of one, or many. And, yes, I will anticipate walking the journey in life by your side. A decree was soon dispatched throughout the land that the prince, and princessa, would be married, and that any subject's, and territory under the tyrant king, are no longer under oppression, and now will be governed by diplomatic rule, also that the two kingdoms, and territories from coast to coast, have been united by an alliance of justice and truth. So it is decreed, with this declaration all aggression against the kingdom ceased, attacking enemies now became a cohesive alliance with the kingdom, bringing peace to the land. The wedding was held on the shore of the sea, with guest from all around. Just off the shore the mermaids and dolphins witness the ceremony, and the wedding gift to the royal couple was that from this day forth, that the dolphins emissaries of the sea, would always be a friend to mankind in service; and that the sea shell's would always give the gift from the ocean with vibration, and song. That's why to this day, if you pick up a sea shell and put it to your ear, you can hear the sound's of the sea.

The Alchemist and The Hypnotist

I'm going to take you to a dark place, you see I have to, in order to take you into the light, it's okay sometimes to be in the darkness for in the darkness you can find solace, find quiet, find stillness.

It is a chill cold cloudy day, and off a snow cover road there's a house that sits just off it, it has smoke coming out of it's chimney, inside there is a family snuggle in it's warmth, with activity around the kitchen, a dad sits at a table and reads the paper, a mother cooking at a stove, two young boys are finishing up their bowls of oat meal anxious to leave, for today these two boys, Billy seven, and Timmy eight years old, have been waiting all week to go on there weekend adventure as the activity increased in the house, there trusted companion poke, the dog lies by the fire place lazily with eyes half closed. As Billy and Timmy are putting on winter coats, gloves and scarfs, their dad puts his paper down to address the boys with his wisdom of caution and, as he speaks, their mother comes to inspect their garments to make sure they're all warm for the outside cold, the father says "now boys, go and have fun, be careful and look out for each other, look, listen, and think, and their mother adds, "be safe," and with that they run for the door outside, with poke close behind barking happily. They run giggling, and smiling to the barn, to grab the sled, and start their joyous journey down the snowy road, along the half mile walk they chirpingly chat with each other as poke barks in agreement every so often, as they *come* to a bend in the road and the panoramic view of the opening, their eyes light up and smiles beam with joy and antici-pation, they see the ice covered lake in all it's beauty of a winter wonderland. The lake is silent, but it's silence roars like an open amusement park with only three allowed to gain entrance, Billy, Timmy and poke run to the edge of ice and do a dive of slip and slide that glides them across the lake like Birds in flight, they crackle with laughter and joy, as they pull each other on there sled. For hundreds of years and seasons, the lake has frozen over and been a point of connection of ice that nature has used in the winter season, but just as seasons change, nature does too, and what once held strong becomes weak, and just as in life some time things crack, chemical, environmental, social, emotional and physically cracking and break due to pressures. And just as one can be at a plateau of joy, spirit, successes, the rupture starts the fissure within begin, and at that moment, as Timmy was pulling Billy on the sled across the lake going in circles, laughing feeling the breath of life at it's greatest, on it's most beautiful day, a moment happens, at first there's the silence, a dispensation, then the chaotic noise of something about to happen, poke barks first as his intuition kicks in then Timmy stops, listens Billy still laughing as he looks into Timmy eye's, and asks "What you stop for?" Just then he hears the deafening crack, crr-ar-arack, as he and the sled slip into the cold darkness of the lake. Timmy starts to run toward him as the rope line of the sled slips from his hand, he runs, but stop as his father's words echo through his head, watch, look, listen but he is frantic as he hears Billy's cries Poke takes off running for the house no other reason than instinct tells him too, Billy tries to grab the edge of the ice, but each time is slipper than the next, and he knows he's losing out, Timmy is scared in fear that he has never known, or felt, even though he can't think intuition makes him look, listen, and as he looks around him at the desolate lake and surroundings all that stands out at the lakes edge is a tree standing twenty-five feet tall, with limbs stretching over the lake fifteen feet long. Everything goes black... The light, intensity, awakening ... "Timmy, Timmy" the EMT's call to him as they shine a pin light into each pupil of his eye's, for Timmy seems to be in a state of deep trance, poke barks in the distance as he stands next to Billy as he is shivering in a protective thermal blanket, as his parents hold each other in fear, and relief, of the event that has happened. Law enforcement and investigators are on the scene also neighbors from near by. Investigators are questioning each other as to what happened, and are perplexed as to how a boy could save his brother. On the icy lake lays a large tree branch weighing over a hundred and fifty pounds detached off the tree that sits on the edge of the bank, the branch was broken off fifteen feet above the ground, investigators are internally and verbally expressing that it's physically impossible for a seven year old boy to have reached up the tree, and broken a hundred and fifty pound branch off and carried over the icy lake to the middle, and use it to save his brother.

Investigators are asking Timmy how he did it, but Timmy just shakes his head, he doesn't remember anything after his brother fell in the water. An old man stands near, smoking his pipe, I can tell you how he did it, he says. "How'd he do it" someone asked then, he did it because no one said he couldn't that's how he did it.